The Right Answer

Siân Lewis

Illustrated by James Field

The Right Answer

My brother Griff didn't come to school on Monday, so he missed all the excitement and the rejoicing. I ran home to tell him about it and met Mam who was walking across the fields with a handful of wild potatoes.

'Where's Griff?' I said.

Mam hesitated and glanced westwards across the pampas.

'Oh!' I snorted. 'It's not fair. He's gone off hunting, hasn't he?'

Mam didn't reply and when I looked round, I saw that Bessie, our mare, was tied to the rail at the side of the house. That's when a knot began to tighten in my stomach.

'Where is he?' I asked.

'Oh Jane, he ran off on his own,' said Mam.

'Ran off?' I said. 'On foot? How long's he been gone?'

'Since this morning,' said Mam.

That morning when we'd got up, Dad was sitting slumped on the yard. He was crying. We had never seen him cry before. He was crying because we had no food to eat. He was crying because he'd brought us out to Patagonia.

Once we lived in Wales in a grey house in a grey street with a narrow strip of sky overhead. My father's face was grey then too – grey and coal-dusty – but his heart was always hopeful. I remember the ringing sound of his hobnailed boots as he came down our street one day and threw his

arms around my mother, my brother and me. People came out onto their doorsteps to listen to his words. 'We four are going to build a new and better life,' my father said proudly. 'We are moving to a new Wales in the wide green spaces of Patagonia.'

It was Edwin Cynrig Roberts who had put the idea into my dad's head. Edwin was a young Welshman who had been brought up in America. When he came to our town, we all crowded into the chapel to hear him speak.

'Welsh men and women have scattered all over the world,' Edwin said in that stirring way of his. 'Poverty and oppression have driven them out of their homeland in search of a new life. But that new life has come at a price. In America, where I live, Welsh people are losing their Welshness. The only answer is to found our own country, a country that will be ours to rule, where even the rivers will sing out in Welsh. The government of Argentina has promised us land in Patagonia. So what are we waiting for? Let's go and possess the land.'

My parents, my brother and I weren't the only ones to respond to Edwin's call. More than a hundred and sixty of us left our homes and our friends, packed what little we owned and set sail for South America aboard the ship Mimosa. We all stood on deck and sang in Welsh as the ship prepared to sail out of the port of Liverpool on the 25th of May 1865, two years ago. On the 28th we were on our way.

What a journey that was. We spent two whole months at sea. Two months was a long time aboard a stuffy old ship, especially with people falling ill all around us and babies dying. The journey would have felt longer still if Dafydd hadn't been there to entertain us.

Dafydd Williams was my brother's hero. Griff used to follow him around like a little pet dog. Dafydd was always so eager and cheerful. He was twenty-one years old and a shoemaker by trade. In his coat he kept a needle, a dented thimble and a little red notebook. The needle and the thimble were to mend the soles of boots, he said, and the notebook was to help poor souls who were bored.

Whenever Dafydd took out his red notebook, we children would gather around him. Then he would ask us questions or riddles like this:

'A baby was born in a house in Llan-gan
Who wasn't a son to his dad or his mam.
He wasn't the son of a man or a god
But that baby was normal and not at all odd.
Why not?'

That riddle puzzled me a bit when I first heard it. But when you think about it, it's obvious. The baby was a girl!

Griff used to sit down right next to Dafydd and mouth the questions with him. Then he'd shout out the answers louder than anyone. He even made a notebook out of some scraps of paper that Mam had given him and made a list of Dafydd's questions so he could learn the answers off by heart.

But there were three questions he didn't need to write

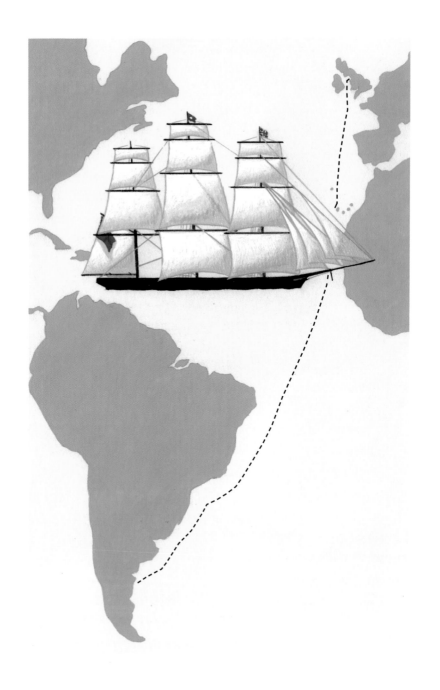

down. Everyone knew the answers to those three, because Dafydd used to ask them regularly at the end of every session. He'd wink at us over the top of the notebook, then we'd all fall silent and suck in our breath. Above us the grey old sails of the Mimosa would huff and puff. Around us the decks would creak and the waves would slap. But we wouldn't hear a thing. All eyes would be fixed on Dafydd.

'Now then,' Dafydd would say, 'here's a very important question. Think carefully before you answer. Which country…which country is the best in the world?'

'Patagonia!' we roared louder than the wind.

'Which country is heaven on earth?'

'Patagonia!'

'Where are we going to build a green and beautiful new Wales?'

'Patagonia!'

When the noise died down, Dafydd's round cheery face would beam at us.

'Well done,' he would say. 'Quite right.'

But it wasn't 'quite right'. Far from it.

On the 28th of July 1865 my parents, Griff and I, along with our friends, set foot on the soil of Patagonia for the very first time. July is summer in Wales. In Patagonia it's winter. A cold, biting rain was falling as we stepped ashore. Edwin Roberts and our leader, Lewis Jones, had gone on ahead to prepare for our arrival. We expected homes that would shelter us, but Edwin and Lewis had run into all sorts of problems and so the only completed building on that

bleak stony beach was a long wooden shed. As we huddled among our belongings on the shingle, my mother wept. I can still hear the panic in her voice and the terrible wail she gave when my brother ran across the beach to look at the land beyond the shore.

'Griff! Griff! Griff!' she called. 'Come back! Come back!'

She was afraid for him.

We were all afraid.

It wasn't just the rain and lack of shelter that scared us. Something terrible had happened.

The day before we landed, when the Mimosa was anchored out in the bay, Edwin Roberts had rowed out to greet us, and Dafydd and some of his friends had insisted on going ashore with him that very day. They were so eager and excited they couldn't wait to set eyes on the green and pleasant land of Patagonia. Poor boys! What a disappointment lay in store for them. The land was not green. It was not pleasant. From the beach all you could see was miles and miles of dusty desert sprinkled with thorn bushes.

So what did Dafydd do? He ran on. We had never intended to settle right on the coast anyway. The government of Argentina had given us land on the banks of the river Chupat, or Camwy, as we now know it. So Dafydd had left his companions. He had run on in the hope of finding this fine new land. By the time the rest of us came ashore the following day, he was lost.

We never saw him again, so we knew he must have

died. Griff, though, insisted that Dafydd had kept on running and running till he found that beautiful green place somewhere far to the west of us. We never had the heart to argue with him. We should have. We should have told him straight.

As I walked home with Mam on Monday, I slid my arm around her waist.

'Griff'll soon be back,' I said.

But I couldn't be sure.

I'd felt so happy coming home from school that day. Thanks to our neighbours Rachel and Aaron Jenkins, everyone was happy. You see, our land is so dry, that the crops have always wilted in the fields. That's why we've all been starving. But over the weekend Rachel and Aaron had worked out an efficient way of irrigating the land. They'd found the answer to our problems.

Mam and Dad had already heard the news and Dad had gone rushing down to the Jenkins's farm to see the miracle for himself. Mam and I should have followed him, but instead we stood in the yard, while the potatoes cooked on the fire, and watched the steam drift out across the pampas.

'Griff knows the pampas well,' I said.

'Then why hasn't he come back?' said Mam. 'He took no food with him. And I've been worried about him over this past month. He's been so quiet, not his usual self at all.'

I tried to think back. For the past month I'd been so hungry that I could think of no one but myself. But Mam

was right. Of the four of us my brother is the only one who really loves Patagonia. He's the one who's always reminding us of its good points. 'We've got our own houses and our own land, which we never would have had in Wales,' he says. 'We've got a school where we're taught in Welsh. We've got our eisteddfod and our chapel and we can do things our own way.' When we tried to pack up and move away some months ago, Griff was the one who was glad we turned back. But for the past weeks there had been a sadness and a shiftiness about him that was more than just hunger.

'You don't think he's been planning to run away?' I said. 'Where would he go to?'

My mother shrugged.

'He's never grown out of that dream, has he?' she said. 'That dream we all had when we came here. He still thinks there's a corner of Patagonia that's green and pleasant.'

'You think he's run off like…Daf…?' I was scared to say the young shoemaker's name.

I was more scared still, when Mam bit her lip and didn't answer.

I turned again to look westward across the pampas.

'I'll saddle up Bess,' I said stoutly. 'I'll soon find him and bring him back.'

'No, Jane,' my mother said, but the 'no' was half-hearted.

How could you find one skinny little twelve-year-old boy in a space that was so big? My mother knew it was impossible, but still she let me go. She touched me with a hand that was as hard as the earth. Her face is hard too,

except when she laughs in her sleep. In her sleep she is back home milking the cows with her brothers and sisters in Wales.

To make her laugh I whirled my hand through the air. 'I'll get myself a bolas,' I said, 'and I'll catch him with it.'

She smiled. A bolas is a rope with a weight at each end of it. The Indians send it flying through the air to catch animals. They've taught Griff how to use it, though all he's caught so far is a fence post.

I got on Bessie's back and whooped just for show. Our bony old mare bucked at the noise and cantered off in quite a sprightly fashion. I didn't look back till we'd gone half a mile, and my mother was still there, a thin shadow in the yard.

Why did Griff have to run off and ruin that day of all days?

Life is cruel. Patagonia can be cruel. In the two years we've been here so many people have died. Lewis Jones has left us to go to Buenos Aires, but Edwin Roberts is still here and always hopeful.

My brother has a hopeful face too. If I closed my eyes, I could see it before me. But when I opened them, there was nothing there, only thorn bush, and the twitch of a hare that, like us, was trying to scavenge a living from the soil.

It was useless. As I rode across the pampas sometimes I drove Bessie on in a fury. Sometimes my heart beat so hard I had no breath left and then I had to pull on the rein to slow the horse. My sweat mingled with the animal's sweat and its breath and mine were all I could hear beneath the

vastness of the sky. Once a pale blur moved soundlessly against the horizon, but it was only a herd of guanaco. At first we used to call them 'red sheep', though their necks and legs are far too long.

I whispered Griff's name. Then I felt ashamed of my own hopelessness and shouted at the top of my voice. As I shouted, I felt vibrations in the earth and saw a dust cloud rolling across the pampas. It was a group of Indians galloping straight towards me. I thought their horses would trample me with their flashing hoofs, but their riders brought them to a halt a short distance away. There were two older men wrapped in cloaks and two young boys. They were on their way to trade with us and had brought along two spare horses with leather and mats and ponchos strapped to their backs.

I greeted them with the few words of Spanish I knew. The Indians have their own language, just as we have, but Spanish is the language of Argentina.

They nodded and watched me.

'I am looking for Griff,' I said. Griff and his friends had been out hunting with the Indians many times. 'Griff,' I repeated.

'Griff,' the younger boy said.

'You've seen him?' I asked.

The boy stared.

'I am looking for Griff now,' I said, making a show of shading my eyes and peering around me. 'I am looking for Griff.'

The Indians talked amongst themselves, then the boy

came towards me and pointed in a south-easterly direction. I had started to turn the horse around, so we could head that way, when I realised he was making the sign of the cross.

In my alarm I gave such a sharp tug on the rein that Bessie whinnied and shied away. As I fell against her neck, the boy made the sign of the cross again and this time he pointed to the ground, as though to a grave.

'Why are you making that sign?' I cried, snatching at Bessie's mane. 'What's happened to Griff? Where is he?'

My shouting had startled the boy. When I reached out my hand to calm him, he backed away and returned to his companions.

'Don't go!' I begged. 'I've got to find my brother. I've got to find Griff.'

The Indians rode away with a murmur of voices. I urged Bessie on. Bony and thin as she was I'd have made her gallop like the wind in pursuit of them, but the boy had paused and was looking over his shoulder at me.

'Griff,' he said and he rode away from his companions.

I followed. I had never made such a terrible journey. When we first arrived in Patagonia, we had to trek through thirty-five miles of thorn bush to reach the patch of land that was ours. I know our parents were scared then and their hearts were breaking, but at least we took some comfort in reaching the ruins of the old fort where we set up our first home. Now I didn't want to reach anywhere.

I was so afraid of what I would find, I wanted to ride on forever till the sun melted me. But, as Mam says, this

land doesn't bend to your wishes. After only a few minutes Bessie stumbled into a hollow and threw me from the saddle. I landed heavily on the ground, and when I sat up my arms were sticky with blood and dust. I brushed the dust away and looked for cuts on my skin, but there were none. The blood wasn't mine. As I jumped to my feet, the Indian boy came back to me and pointed at a dark patch that was seeping into the soil.

'Griff,' he said and he nodded towards a ridge a short distance away.

I turned my head. At the foot of the ridge was a mound of earth. On the mound stood a cross of twigs and on top of the cross a tiny light glowed.

In a daze I heard the Indian gallop away. I tried to take a step towards what I thought was my brother's grave, but fell to the ground. As I fell, I heard a voice call my name.

'Jane,' it called. 'Jane! Jane!'

I thought I was dreaming, but footsteps came running up. A hand snatched at mine and there was my brother standing over me, wide-eyed and breathless.

'Jane, what are you doing here?' he asked.

In a moment I was on my feet, ready to throw my arms around him. The next moment I was so angry, I shook him.

'What am I doing here?' I snapped at him. 'What are you doing here is what I want to know.'

'I came to find food for us,' my brother said, and pointed hurriedly at the body of a wild duck that was

spilling blood on the ground.

'But why did you have to run off like that without a word? Mam's sick with worry and it's lucky Dad's not at home. Why don't you get it into your stupid head that there's nowhere to run to?'

My brother's face grew stubborn.

'I know that,' he replied.

'Oh, do you?' I said. 'Since when?'

Griff's only reply was to run off.

'There you go again,' I screamed and ran after him. I grabbed hold of the tail of his coat and we both fell sprawling. We rolled across the ground and collided with the mound of earth.

My brother was back on his feet in a flash. I caught hold of his ankle so he wouldn't get away but all he did was reach out for the little light on top of the cross. He gathered it up in his hand and held it out to me.

The sight of it took my breath away. On the palm of Griff's hand lay a dented brass thimble newly cleaned and sparkling in the sunlight. Although two years had passed since I had last seen it, I would have known that thimble anywhere.

I glanced at the mound of earth and saw the marks where my brother's hands had patted down the soil. 'Oh, Griff!' I said hoarsely. 'It's Dafydd's grave, isn't it? When did you find it?'

'I found his bones and his thimble,' Griff said. 'And…'

'And you buried him all on your own!' I cried. 'Oh, why didn't you tell us?'

'I didn't want people to know he'd made a mess of things, did I?' Griff replied.

He scared me. He sounded so weary, so broken and so like my father. I wanted to tell him my news to cheer him up, but he turned away and with his foot lifted a large stone that lay at the base of the mound. In the hollow beneath the stone I saw a handful of paper bound in tattered red cloth.

At the sight of that pathetic little bundle tears spattered onto the soil. I didn't even realise they were mine.

'Dafydd must have died of thirst within days of disappearing,' said my brother. 'He never even got as far as the river. He got everything wrong, Jane.'

I shook my head.

'He did!' Griff insisted. 'He got everything wrong…'

'No,' I said, rubbing the tears away. 'No he didn't! Listen to me for once. Listen, Griff.'

I knelt down and took those scraps of paper in my hand. The words had all faded and insects had eaten the leaves till they were fragile and fine as lace. But I didn't need words. I could still hear Dafydd's cheerful voice in my head. I made my voice cheerful too.

'Where are we going to build a green and beautiful new Wales?' I asked my brother.

Griff scowled at me.

'Patagonia!' I said. 'It's true, Griff. It's true.'

And I told him the news.

I told him about Rachel and Aaron's irrigated fields and the green crops that would grow in them. I told him that as soon as we followed their example, we too would have fine harvests, barns bursting with grain and tables laden with food.

As I spoke, I saw the scowl leave my brother's face.

'Ask me that question again, Jane,' he urged. 'Ask me that question again.'

So I did:

'Where are we going to build a green and beautiful new Wales?' I asked.

My brother turned towards Dafydd's grave.

'Patagonia!' he said in a proud, firm voice. And again, whooping and punching the air: 'Patagonia!'

'Well done,' I said to him. 'That's the right answer.'

That evening, during the celebrations at Rachel and Aaron's farm, Griff asked the question once more and, for the first time since we'd left the *Mimosa*, every man, woman and child replied with one voice.

'Patagonia!' we sang out. 'Patagonia!'